For Calder and Finley and their Uncle Justin

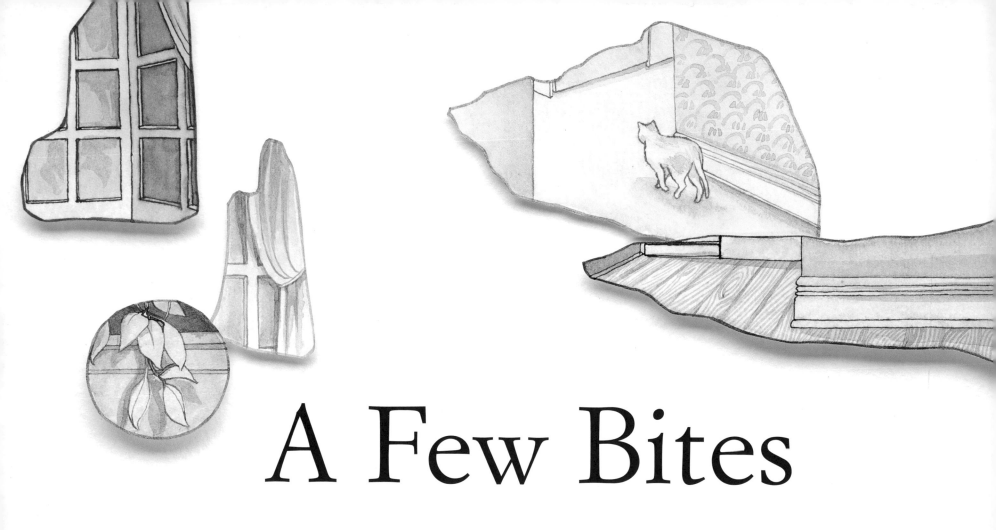

A Few Bites

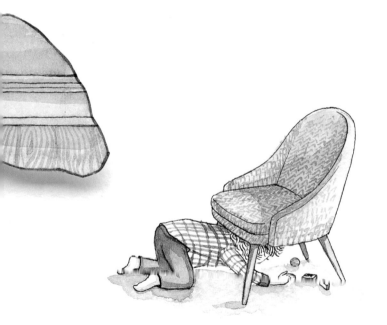

Cybèle Young

Groundwood Books   House of Anansi Press   Toronto   Berkeley

It was time to eat. Viola made lunch for her brother, Ferdie.
It was broccoli, carrot sticks and ravioli.

"Ferdie, come and eat before it gets cold!"
Ferdie was looking for a special part for his fighter ship.
It was gray and square with four bumps on it.

Viola promised to help him find it right after lunch,
so he sat down at the table.

Ferdie scowled at his plate. Pointing to his broccoli, he said, "What's this? I'm definitely not eating it. No, thank you. I'm not even hungry."
"Just try a few bites," pleaded Viola.
But he shook his head.

"That's actually dinosaur food," Viola continued.

"It was around during the Cretaceous, and if you were a dinosaur you would have had to eat five thousand of those broccolis every day."

"That's the only way you would have been strong enough to
climb mountains and scale volcanoes…"

"…and run through dense forests fast enough to escape the fiercest predators."

So the boss decided to come back to the table.

He ate one…　　　　…two…　　　　…three bites.

Ferdie looked at his carrots and sneered.
"I'm absolutely not eating those. Thanks, but no thanks."
He put down his fork.

"I guess you don't want to be like the Zyblot aliens," said Viola.
"They spend their lives searching the galaxy far and wide for one
thing and one thing only…"

"…Orange Power Sticks. Zyblots suck them up through their vacuum trumpets. Then they get super vision and can see past every asteroid, moon and planet in their solar system, way into the next solar system, far, far away."

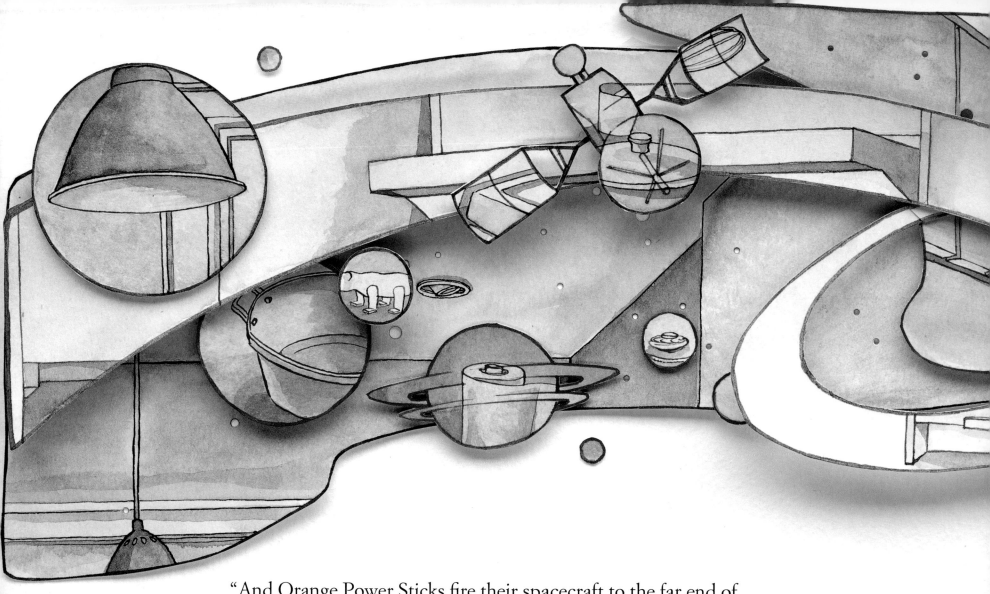

"And Orange Power Sticks fire their spacecraft to the far end of their galaxy, maybe farther, and then all the way back home."

"That's how they plan to dominate the universe."

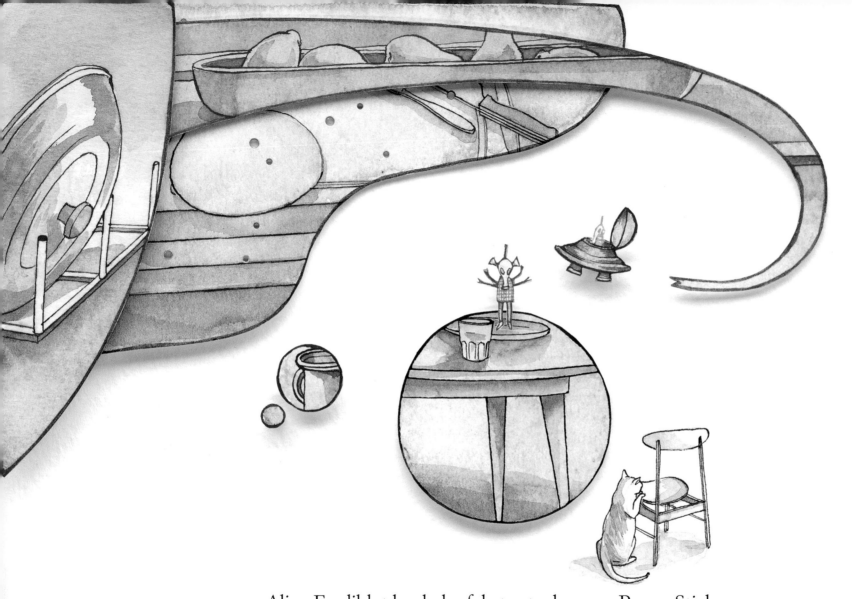

Alien Ferdiblot landed safely to stock up on Power Sticks.

He ate every…   …single…   …one of them.

Ferdie looked at the ravioli. He could see that it was cold.
He looked at Viola.

He looked at the floor and didn't move.

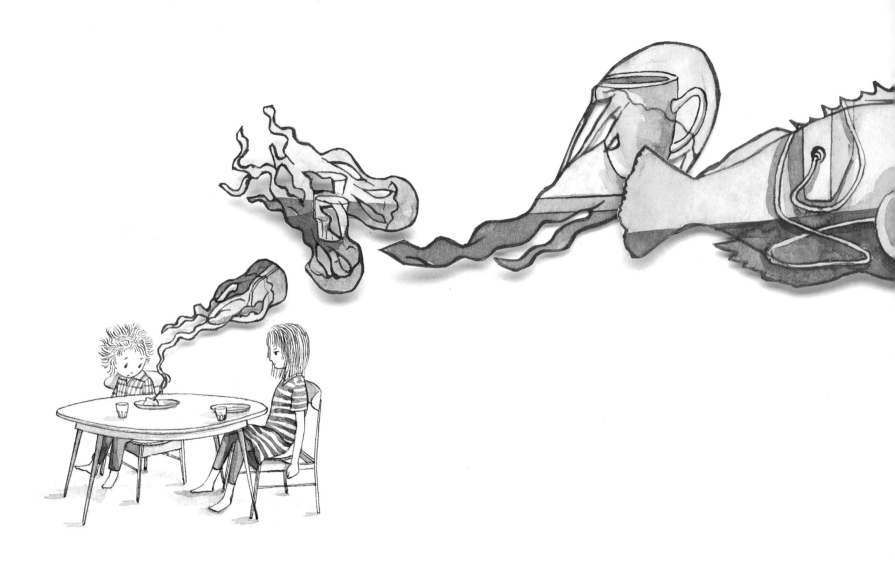

Viola sighed and began, "Deep down in the sea…"

"…ten thousand fathoms at least — darker than any place you've ever known — is buried the key to the greatest mystery in the history of the world."

"He can dodge the wild jelly fishes' sting, swerve around spiked eels and even trick the great glowing devil shark…"

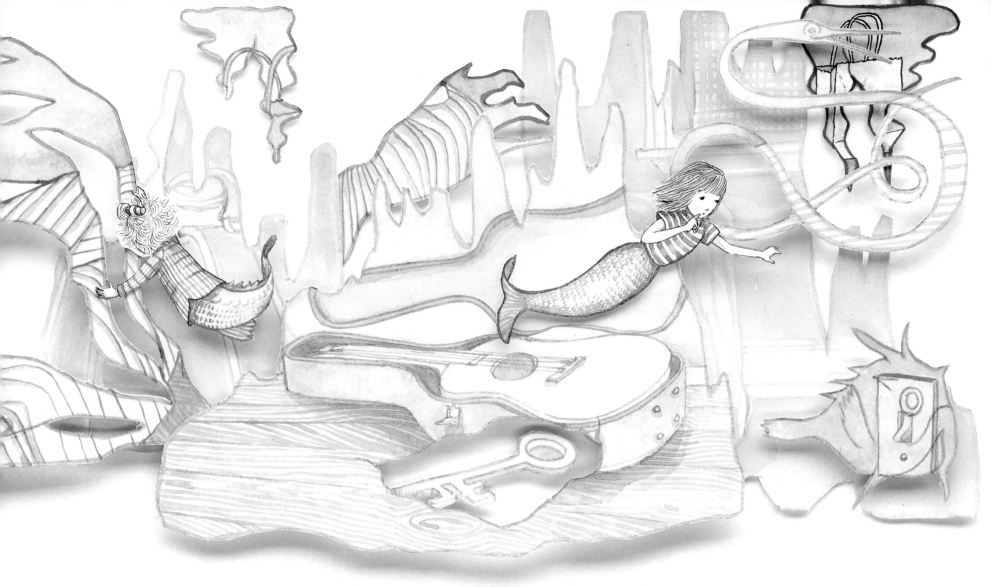

"And when he finds the key…" Viola paused.

"When he finds the key, he…"

"When he finds the key, he does NOTHING and I don't even know what that key is FOR!"

Viola couldn't think of one more thing to say except,
"PLEASE, Ferdie, just finish the last few bites."
Ferdie asked to be excused.

Viola reminded him that he would get no dessert. She plugged in her earphones and sat down, *plop*, in the big armchair.

Ferdie began to sort through his toys. After a while Viola looked up.

"What are you making?" she asked.

"It's a strawberry, chocolate swirl, caramel explosion surprise cake with extra whipped cream and a cherry on top."

"*Mmmm*. Sounds good. Can I have some?"

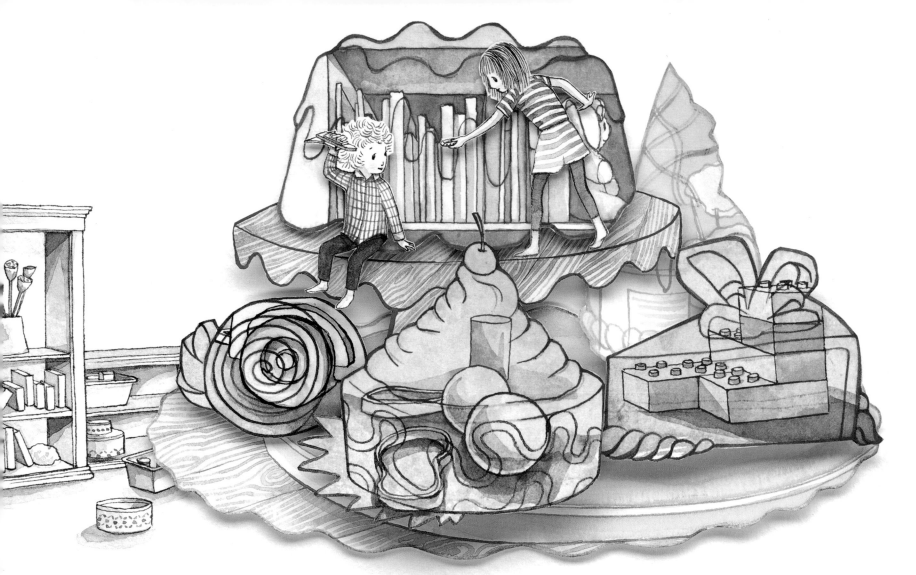

They each had a few bites.
Then Viola said, "Ferdie, let's find that special part
for your fighter ship."